The Bourgeois Empire

Dani & Julie

Literary dames

with admiration ♡

XO Evie

The
Bourgeois
Empire

—

Evie Christie

MISFIT

ECW Press

Published by ECW Press
2120 Queen Street East, Suite 200, Toronto, Ontario, Canada M4E 1E2
416.694.3348 / info@ecwpress.com

LIBRARY AND ARCHIVES CANADA CATALOGUING IN PUBLICATION

Christie, Evie, 1979-
The bourgeois empire / Evie Christie.

ISBN 978-1-55022-935-6

1. Title.

PS8605.H745B68 2010   C813'.6   C2010-901258-5

Editor for the press: Michael Holmes / a misFit book
Cover design: David Gee
Text design: Tania Craan
Typesetting: Mary Bowness
Printing: Coach House   1   2   3   4   5

The publication of *The Bourgeois Empire* has been generously supported
by the Canada Council for the Arts, which last year invested $20.1 million in writing
and publishing throughout Canada, by the Ontario Arts Council, by the
Government of Ontario through the Ontario Book Publishing Tax Credit, by the
OMDC Book Fund, an initiative of the Ontario Media Development Corporation,
and by the Government of Canada through the Canada Book Fund.

  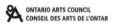

PRINTED AND BOUND IN CANADA

ECW PRESS
ecwpress.com

It is perfectly true that life must be understood backwards. But philosophers tend to forget that it must be lived forward, and if one thinks over that proposition it becomes clear that at no particular moment can I find the necessary resting place from which to understand it backwards.

— Søren Kierkegaard

I have a good heart, but I am a monster.

— Jean Cocteau

CONTENT

Acknowledgements

Thank you to my friends who have read and encouraged (or discouraged) me. Thank you again to my wonderful editor Michael Holmes and to ECW Press.

Thank you to my family: my parents, Karen Christie and Bill Clarke, Mark Christie and Jeanne Brown; my brother, Caleb Christie, and my sister, Rachel Christie-Nichols.

To my daughter, apple of my eye, Harper June, all of my love. To her father, Aaron Allard, my gratitude for your imperial friendship.

For Guy

CHAPTER ONE

Richard, My Man

THE ROOM IS SPINNING OUT OF CONTROL. No, the car, the car is spinning out of control. Wake up, you cocksucker—"cocksucker," even in your best dreams—your life is about to end. Head tilted up between downy teenage tits, waiting for the wreck on the gorgeous flat-screen, anything but this, he slides the head of his penis over her clammy vaginal lips and onto her stomach. He doesn't think: Who is this girl? He thinks: Please God let me wake up. Never come inside a girl who is not your wife. Never penetrate anyone but your wife.

When you met Nadine she was twenty-one and married to her father's friend Richard. You'll never be like Richard, no one will, Richard is the man, don't think about Richard when you come. You were taken with her, staying up all night together doing blow off the White Album with two TVs on pay-per-view channels—not even sex, just that . . . just talking, and maybe sex as well, but afterwards. You talked and Nadine said she thought sex was the act of penetration—you heard her say that. And Richard, he could have been your father, a better-dressed successful father, a father that could, let's face it, never exist. He took you under his tailored wing, introduced you to some nice ass, which at the time was forty-something mind-blowing ass usually, and an all right job with decent money. Then you cut his grass—don't think of Richard.

And then there's God, that antisocial fuck, who wakes you from the dream: the one act of grace in your entire God-fearing life. There is no girl and no four-hour McQueen afternoon double-bill, and in this life you always come inside the girl. You have never been in love with Nadine, it was just sex like anything else, and then a job and money—and money is good and so was Nadine. In this life you don't even want to choose between reality and dreams, either will do, and that's what it is, a hemorrhaging of tits and ass and gold-leaf RSVPs, sticky bills and place card dinner parties—the oppressive lack of love between you and Nadine that, odds on, everyone around you senses, and that's why you have less friends sending idiotic get-well cards with silly costumed cats, or dropping in on a Saturday breakfast with their bloated children of dubious parentage. They are noticeably absent this year, they slowly fly away to vacation homes and tennis courts you've never even seen, buzzing a waspy hatred that really only ever reaches a passive-aggressive hum.

Either nightmare will do: you used to want to wake up as anyone else . . . a labourer in the Negev with no phone number. Jenny took you there, that aggressive lower-middle-class goddess who gave you crabs. You might have fucking murdered her if it hadn't been for her predisposition to pinko political brilliance. She could talk and it was good, better than it should have been. But then eventually you would find a way out of the desert and back here and life would be the same except you would be worse off, having gotten used to something else, something better by any middle-class standard.

The thing to do was to get along, quietly, doing this. Paying for stuff and standing with the kids for a photo in front of a new vacation home and having sex and working and doing non-needle narcotics and having online sex that makes you feel sick for upward of an hour afterward and taking the boat out sailing with Bern the German Shepherd and reading anything long and arduous, anything ascetic enough to make reading feel utilitarian, not arty.

Everything should stay as it is, or you might lose everything, and that's how it is for everyone.

Today was a day for getting along, liver-healing, a cocktail party and a faster wireless connection that tolerates renovated turn-of-the-century walls and allows Candy Cane (or Coconut?) to become a part of your afternoon ensuite bathroom caucus. Life is not good, but it feels good, *on occasion, baby*, is what you might type.

16

CHAPTER TWO

Charlie, Baby

A GIRL IS A GIRL. You've almost always known that. And it's not simply spiteful machismo—you haven't used the word "cunt" since fifth grade—it's just that most girls really are the same. That need to be your first anything: Is this the first time you've seen *White Christmas* with a babysitter? Buttoned a nurse's blouse with one hand? Fed a landlady's fish? Tucked in a teacher's sheets, hotel-style?

Of everything a girl had over a guy, it was honesty, pre-dominantly, that kept the growing gap between the sexes growing. You'd just never come close to a girl on that one. A girl once told you, very plainly, that you were not handsome—

that was the best advice you've ever been given, because it was true. Girls can be trusted to give it to you straight—they've grown cold-blooded from the scalding-hot truths that busted their darling little-girl egos long ago. The great ones have, at least.

And it *was* advice. Certain facts carry with them obvious choices and, delivered in any tone, force a particular option to present itself. This broad was saying, "You are not handsome, but I sleep with you. You have some kind of *it*." She had something there. As with any *it* one always needed more, and now you had more. You had close to everything. And Charlie.

Without Charlie you really had everything.

But sometimes a girl isn't just a girl. Charlie ignited in you a mugger's eye for swag, the jailbird's delusions of freedom. She was also a charming little nerve-wracking cunt who threatened the peace and quiet of your relentlessly rock-steady life.

It wasn't her fault, she said. During her conception, a major American city was being destroyed. Six feet of it under water, and what remained was in flames or being pillaged. Media coverage blossomed in SUVs at the outskirts; police hovered in fat black helicopters, fearing the locals more than the weather.

The world would not be remembering a beloved sitcom star, syndicated TV legend Charlie Hughes, as it might have had he had the good fortune of foresight, and blown his brains out a few days—maybe a week—earlier. No, they would be earnestly shock-peddling, volunteering, doing community activism-ish things.

None of this *explains* anything about Charlie's seeding, her beginnings. People weren't having more sex, huddling together in the dark as they do after terrorist attacks. Or maybe they were, but that is not what I'm getting at. Nine months later (people always say nine but it is more like ten) a city was being rebuilt—celebrities and politicians were cutting things, lighting things, raising hands. Some had written songs, catchy death jingles.

And then—you see where I'm going with this—baby Charlie is born. A woman named Leah Love gives birth under white-hot lights and a cocktail of narcotics. The baby comes into the world sleepy like her mother. Leah looks to the pink fingernail-perforated headlines on the *People* clutched in her left hand and whispers *Charlie baby*. She leaves in the night, taking her bag, the sheets, towels and whatever Demerol she can find in the room under a lighter's guidance. She also finds her roommate's morphine relatively easy to pack. She hasn't left instructions for the nurses who scoff and knot together around the baby, who decide that there is no use trying with some people. And so it is written on the birth certificate, *Charlie Baby Love*.

Don't infer that Charlie was a catastrophe since day one. Yes, she was a stunning example of society's valuing physical beauty over character. She was also, however, reasonably well read and an absolute triumph over her inbreeding. It was her birthright, after all, to enroll in NA, AA—any of the A's really—before her twentieth and to lose two babies to the Children's Aid Society. Still, she was the finest kisser you've ever met, which brands you no less masculine. If anything it makes you even more manly. That thing about kissing, it's spot on.

It's Charlie's fifteenth birthday. You'll have to forget about e-mailing her for now. Block Sender actually—close your laptop and find matching socks for your on-the-mend garden-party bullshit.

CHAPTER THREE

Household Commerce

TO FIND SOCKS, OR ANYTHING ELSE you might want to wear, it would be absolutely necessary to leave your bathroom, your office, your room. You must go downstairs. Usually, in the early morning, it was safe. You could get your coffee and, when you could smoke without being hassled, a pack of cigarettes and some strike-anywheres from above the laundry cupboard. This was not morning, though; it was most definitely early afternoon. Therefore it could not be considered safe. "The family" had become a single, homogenous unit, occupying the same space in your mind—in the world, quite possibly. When distressing occasions of unplanned proximity occurred there was not much to say. You always said *something* though. You were not someone who ignored your family the way some guys do. If you could walk through the house as the invisible man, life would be closer to comfortable. But the younger girl-child always heard you or the sounds your more aggressive habits make.

"Hi, hey." She says something of this nature.

Why not say the same kind of thing back?

Why not say something else?

"What's this?"

Don't close your eyes and make an expression that can only be read as anguish—cut and run, there's still time.

And just as you swivel and begin to walk away, imagining she had not heard you, she answers: "I'm doing paint-by-number. It's my own thing; I draw something and section it out with a black ballpoint pen and then I randomly add the numbers. See?"

She motions toward the patterned sketch that threatens the cherry-stained table beneath.

Does she want an answer? Is this an okay time to opt out of further discussion? Better be safe.

"Good stuff."

"Yeah. So I insert the numbers arbitrarily and then I add colour depending on this number and colour legend I made." She's pointing to the bottom of the paper, at what looks like the legend on the early world map hanging above the highboy.

For Christ's sake, that's both so dull and irrational it demands a follow-up.

"Why?"

"It looks cool," she almost whispers, deep in concentration, without looking up from the lacklustre, mostly water watercolour.

"But you are the one who *made* the picture. You *must* know, even subconsciously, the variables in the colour-number scheme. What's the point?"

She looks vaguely confused. "It looks nice, right?"

And now you see there really is no point continuing. "Tell your mother I'm working all afternoon."

You slip away. If it were not for the aging soles of your beaded leather slippers (which are not yuppie exoticism, as native art by definition cannot really be deemed "exotic"— besides you've had them since your terrible twenties) scratching at the hardwood, it would have been a classic invisible man maneuver. You think about turning back to say something more. That particular piece of furniture was given to you, to both of you, as a wedding gift. It is irreplaceable.

Who gave it to you, you wonder as you slip up the staircase, a heavily burdened man in a pilled robe and moccasins?

CHAPTER FOUR

CEO, T&A

UPSTAIRS. The closest to thing to asylum you can attain. Not John List solitude—people may still be moving, making noises below. But there is a comforting degree of sound-proofing and a rather handy vestige of the previous and, if workmanship is any indication, unequivocally superior, century, in a functioning key-lock door. Unsafe in an inferno, they say, but safer for everyone, really, fire-safety aside. It wasn't as though you were doing horrible things; it was simply a matter of etiquette. You were extending privacy to the entire household, a gesture that kept everything running A-okay. There are lines you do not cross: needles, bestiality, hugs, kissing untidy girls, relations with relations (no matter how close or distant they may be).

Staying within the lines had become increasingly less difficult, as the lines were ever-changing. Age, for instance, mattered less and less. It started with pay sites, those uninspired pros working old, hard cocks to grey death. And then, the evolution: the unfathomable scope of torrents unfolded, click after melodious click. Who were these girls? You never asked. But how old? Yeah, maybe you asked that—it just wasn't clear. It became meaningless, the lines had blurred. Was *barely legal* 25 or 16? As their moral guidelines altered so did yours. It was a mutually beneficial relationship, right? This dialogue you had was all right: "Find me someone I'd like to fuck"—and, blip!

A curiously weak blip at that.

That served your needs mostly. But there were times when you'd like to talk to someone about something, the commissioner of pornography, someone who knew the whole deal. Especially today, you've taken the time to search for amateur porn, you don't have all the fucking time in the world and yet you don't have the stomach for *14 y o has sex with older brother* and maybe that's your problem. Makes you think there needs to be some kind of advisory board for what passes as amateur. This clearly was not it. The couple moves from place to place, unrehearsed? You guess it was possible. When did your sex life become so static? It seemed to start and end in the same location lately—lately being the last ten years. Perhaps it was unrealistic to believe a man could be at the top of his game after so much time, so many years with the confinements of refinement—the wife, the silk ties, the furniture, the things you didn't want to damage, things you were careful with.

Were your own parents expected to slog off a bang between breakfast and brunch? No, they were not. They weren't even expected to know what the *Times* had to say that *week*; they were not expected to get involved in anyone else's business but their own. And your parents had each other in their pithy existence, which was *something*. Your parents were still married the last time you saw them, not so long before their death as rumour had it. They had two children before they were twenty-five and raised them in a small village in northern Toronto, without incident. Then *you* are born, into a family who does not expect a baby, your mother being forty years old and past what she (and maybe you) considered the "child-bearing years." You are born quietly into a quiet family. You don't cry, they tell you—maybe because you felt it would upset someone. What you learn about silence is taken from others: getting anything done means it's a necessity. What you learn about silence is that it isn't about what you're not saying at that moment, but what you've always wanted to say or—for a long time, probably, and at this rate—never will.

You were brought home from the hospital in an adult towel and you slept in a bed in a small room and not a crib. There was no crib available. It was probably given away a long time ago. You might ask, what is the point in remembering? As you do when a memory so crudely and violently hauls you back into that district—a panelled landing maybe, a carpeted staircase—where someone calls out telling you not to forget something that you will inevitably forget. A district where your seedy heart is threaded—with a fine but tough string—to everything else around it. (Everything, even that which it hates more than anything else.) Can you escape? You have escaped, haven't you? You might look down now and notice, among other things, that you are not ready. And how hot the room is getting.

CHAPTER FIVE

Ballpark Figure

IF THIS ROOM DID CATCH ON FIRE, with the computer jammed and not turning off, no matter how many times you *Ctrl-Alt-Deleted* or how firm and steadfast you are with the on/off button, would you burn with it? Do you hope your robe abides, drape yourself over the screen? Hope a testical doesn't drop aside, remaining evermore (God help us) your younger daughter's first sighting (you'd given up on the older) of the saddest of male anatomy, the cowardly half-formed unit of masculinity, keeper of life—the balls? Yeah, you guess so. And what would they say of your body after some lean VFDD kid hacked through the oak door to revive you? *There was a middle-aged man grotesquely guarding his LCD screen?* That's the best-case scenario. It could be *fat old man*, or *heavy-set half-naked guy*, or *out-of-shape, middle-aged, spindle-legged* . . . There was nothing particularly *great* that could be said. Your insides, though, they must be all right, right? An occasional Scotch bender (though this was much less feasible since your surgery) and a smoke here and there, but mostly things were on the up and up—the cost of living, you know, is high: doing shit you don't want to do, including eating things you didn't like, exercising in ways you didn't enjoy, and abstaining from whatever vices made you feel, momentarily, okay about the world.

You had an awfully fine naturopathic doctor ballpark it one afternoon, and she thought you could live past seventy-three. At the time you went into a ruthless depression about dying before 100, but right now, as the room gets hotter, it seems golden, that seventy-three. Inside you should be all right. What about the heart, the stress and lack of sleep? Charlie—her legs alone! Your heart probably wasn't anything to write home about—the word "clotted" comes to mind. That wasn't the heart though, was it? The arteries. But the heart, still: fat, hair-trigger, coagulated, foul. These were stored adjectives; you weren't just composing them on the fly. Once, five or ten years ago, when you were still into making it work, being a better man, your new-age psychologist asked what your heart would feel like, how it would smell and taste. You hoped it would taste gamey and you said so, but you thought others would say it was tough, overcooked, dead stock. That's not what she'd been looking for. She wanted it to be an orange with cloves piercing its brawny myocardium, a candy apple with a tiny wormhole bored through its core. She was, I think we can all agree on this now, a *bona fide* nutcase.

Since then it's been frank analysis, a neologism that, to you, meant ultra-clinical psychiatric treatment, and an aggressive prescription-med regimen, off and on. Most recently very *off*.

Less embarrassing than being rescued from your own office with a visible torrent storm freezing up your screen, you find yourself waking twenty minutes later, without injury, still mildly scraping at the door, the remarkably unscathed door. A mild heart attack? Possibly, but more likely a pill-less panic attack, something that could get you a new scrip, something that could, for the moment, be swept under the Persian rug.

Of course, you stupid cock, unplug the system. It should have been obvious. But you had trained yourself in the art of the ever-ready lie, the at-all-costs cover up, and you were good. Usually. The thought of being "caught" at anything, even a pale lie, was unbearable.

One crack and the walls would surely cave in.

CHAPTER SIX

High as a Kite

A SON IS SOMETHING DIFFERENT ENTIRELY. Imagine it—you hadn't—someone like you, in a way, only enhanced, someone who usurped and made redundant, obsolete, your every move and breath. This is the natural history of the son. The rest? Categorically storybook, ball-throwing-and-catching bullshit. Alistair developed from a toddler into a man in a matter of moments. Your corporate years were measured like this: one year equalled five of other people's years. Your people's lives happening, in lightning-bolt episodes, at some distance.

So Alistair had grown into a man. He was "male" in the

decent sense of the word— strong, lean, a perfect mix of Wasp and Semitic bone and blood and hair. Smart, funny, and probably "caring and supportive." One of those guys, you imagined. He was never any trouble—meaning, Nadine never bothered you with anything about him in the evening. He was always busy and active, as though he were your mirror opposite, if such a thing existed, as though everything he did was a tyrannical blow thumping you in the chest and making you sweaty and nauseous and sad. His polite wave as he went out the door; his cheerful *See you there* that night could only be met with a *mm-hmm*, something that embarrassed you, and yet how could you help it? You hadn't been sleeping, you weren't yourself, and something (everything) about him bothered you. You didn't want to go, remember? You didn't want to go.

Of course you remember, you remember it almost every day.

A school fundraiser? The details were not clear. Something like this was going on, a variety show is what they used to call them, a talent show. Alistair would read from his naive and, according to everyone, otherwise pretty good short story; a fat Ruskie kid dances (they are not called *Ruskies*, says Nadine); a mildly entertaining stand-up act that includes a lot of material that upsets the crowd, the faculty, the exchange students and the mascot. The mascot overheats and passes out during the cheer that explodes after the many PC apologies. A group of desperately obese and ill-clothed teachers and some choice look-alikes from the student body perform a hopelessly pathetic version of a popular hip-hop song. The level of activity, how agile these people are, mesmerizes you. Will they be hurt, you remember wondering. Will they be hurting later tonight, pointed quietly at an episode of *Millionaire*, over Lean Cuisine dinners followed by a whole low-fat cake, something sticky and processed and demoralizing? After the next act your memory becomes a queasy mash-up: listening to a one-man play about bullying, the one man looking incredibly bully-able, driving home, almost hitting a dog or a child near your driveway, going out to smoke and giving Nadine some tax files. The dead end and the girl. And the high wire.

No one does the tightrope circus spiel anymore, except maybe high-grade specialist strippers. But the most extraordinary thing about the highwire act, aside from the many safety violations that had to be occurring with each step, was the lack of overt stripper-esque sexuality. A girl with brown hair hanging to her shoulders, longish bangs over her eyes, a blue T-shirt and boyish flood-ready jeans, bare feet, not looking particularly focused, not looking as though she has any real need to get across the rope. At one point you are certain she will walk back the way she came and sit down on the ladder until everyone leaves, but she was merely going back for her gun. A pearl-handled sidearm like the one holstered in buckskin with jade studs on her other hip. In the middle of the rope she fixes her hair, continues, takes a pronounced bow then exits stage right, pointing her gun at whoever was waiting for her. Why had she even needed the guns? She had it, raw power (you) in the palm of her hand. *What a theatrical little bitch*, you think now as you remember it once more.

It would be a lie to say that night was the first time you'd driven your Audi to the dead end of the cul-du-sac to jerk off in private. It was just that particular hour of the evening, a muffled drone of familial activity, distractions. Even the faintest sound would blow your five minutes of manly behaviour. The street was dark and lush, the interior leather coolish and uncomfortable. For the next week you eyed the gearshift and dash for evidence of your happiness while a woman, wife or daughter, spoke about something next to you.

There was a sense of excitement about everything, analogous to your early years when a female cousin showed up at a party and then ended up spending the night, a cousin you never knew you had and never knew you wanted to fuck until she walked in the door, then for the rest of your visit you were consumed with only that—there was only so much time. But more than that, the girl had something. She looked like a girl who could roll a perfect cigarette, who would teach you how to concoct the perfect speedball, who would read in bed for half the day and smoke the other half. What made you nervous about her? She was a girl after all, and weren't girls mostly the same? She was man-cool, was that it? The women you knew had all been decidedly uncool. They were other things: smart, weird, sexy, funny—but not cool, at least not this calibre of cool. Cool had been everything to your generation, it was steadfast and definable; it was physical. What did it really take? Jeans? Good hair. Boots. Your body, in its actual, natural state. Music, parties, personality (almost any would be sufficient). Drugs. Alcohol. Now it seemed as though cool was immaterial, vague and in constant flux. It was at times the opposite of itself and made you think, *makes* you think: *How does anyone get laid on the straight anymore?* Cool was lost and the only man who ever pulled it off anymore was maybe Bruce Springsteen. Don't even try, your mirror has often reminded you. Please don't try. It won't end well.

You can usually duck in through the back door, mumbling something about Bern and a raccoon, brushing at your pants, and be free, slipping away in a cloud of "I'd better get out of these clothes and back to work." When you get to the bathroom mirror you notice your breath, unusually spirited and strong, refusing to give in to its natural enemy, you, your body, your habits. It's all too wonderful, a good-ish feeling. Virility? Post-masturbatory hormonal contentment?

No, it was real. Could it be real?

Was she real? She was real, the girl standing over your toilet. Not standing—*straddling.* A better word for what was happening.

CHAPTER SEVEN

Bloody Heaven

SHE'S THERE IN YOUR BATHROOM WHEN YOU GET HOME, naked from the waist down. (Always a surprising way to encounter someone.) Is she shoving something in? Remembering is half the heartache: a tampon and blood, an unsurprised-looking young girl, pantless. "Hello" is the way you began, the manner in which you were, as a man, born again. "I didn't know anyone was here." It went something like this. It went like it did in 1982 when your friend Chris Morris was hit by a car—worse, a VW Rabbit. Fuckers. A slightly less than active man was transformed, performing something close to a back flip. Landing and then moving, almost jauntily, to the side of the road. The shock mechanism: everything inside bashing against itself, the body and the brain trading places. The body, for once in its life, taking over, rationally, beautifully, performing as one might expect it to if one still had expectations, mature as it had never been. The brain, frozen, retarded momentarily: always trying to outstrip, sending its hundred or trillion signals, protecting itself from its warden, the madman, you.

This is what Chris had said in 1982. Or, as you remembered it, this is what was happening. Shock mechanism, meaning you didn't cry or try to fondle the naked ass before you, close and accessible as it was. You apologized, swivelled, reached into your drawer for the Scotch, wondered if young girls drank Scotch, wondered if this was a young girl. You still did wonder that: How young?

It was her.

"I'm Charlie. Sorry for the crime scene. I found these tights in the hall cupboard." She waits for your response, holding up the aforementioned tights with a crooked almost-smile.

"And I'm taking someone's panties. They are cotton and bright-white-white—so I'm assuming they belong to an elderly nurse who may live on the premises."

She smiles as though she imagined you'd need to stop yourself from breaking into laughter.

But this is where you may have potted your fate, being strong and composed and stern, something that betrayed your every male cell and was in keeping with nothing you'd done before.

"I think we both know those belong to my wife."

"I *am* sorry." The emphasis was more than a little insulting coming from someone grinning so hard.

Charlie was, and remains, the kind of girl who could make you viciously frustrated in a matter of moments with as little as a slight modification in her expression. Luckily. Luckily because otherwise you may have been provoked to plead with her to stay the night—the menstrual situation noted but overlooked as an undeniable yet compelling (entertaining?) snag en route to sexual intercourse. The conversation went on like this, poorly, muted. Both of you aware that you didn't want to alert anyone else of your presence together, this private and violent intimacy. Things progressed, naturally and climactically as all great fights do. It was, the narrator seems to be saying, a shocking and unexpected bit of fun in its sheer and unrestrained aggression. The past twenty years of your life had convinced you that passive aggression was the accepted and appropriate modus operandi for humanity. Lovers and friends hadn't been known to blacken each other's eyes as of late, instead they administered the equivalent, modern beat-down, with costly and tedious legal proceedings. Charlie was (and continues to be) asking for a bloody lip at least twenty-five percent of the time. She offered, liberally and gladly, the promise of actual physical and emotional transactions—evidence, as it would soon and often become clear, that she was the one you wanted.

"Because you are in what is as good as my own fraction

of this house I think I have the right to ask you to leave."

"Oh. Okay." Still smiling; more teeth.

"You're an asshole." Had you really said this? In hindsight, you were of course much cooler. Aren't we all?

"Girls, traditionally, are not referred to as 'assholes,' you know. Bitch, cunt, that sort of thing is more in keeping with the normal, or modern, vernacular."

So you *had* said it, clearly.

With this, her response, your heart was stolen, a thumping bloody mess.

Cunt, cold and Germanic. She used it beautifully, technically, all the while remaining courteous in tone, never compromising charm for vulgarity or vice. Perhaps this is where other girls hadn't won your loyalty or interest even. Their embarrassment with every single non-maternal or career- or lifestyle-centric thing they had done. It left a relationship lacking. And those who did not operate with shame as a motivational pal behaved in a demonstratively harsh and masculine manner. It was all so unbearably dull. Not so with our Charlie, never a moment's rest, never a moment without the sense of a consequence approaching, just off in the distance. You feel it don't you? The next weeks and months are the only ones worth remembering, if the 800 plus e-mails and hundred or thousand hours of instant messaging were a gauge of self-fulfillment, love, exultation. Transcendence? (That was your boyhood coming through, and it wasn't really true.) Let's just say it was a good time; the girl was wonderful, brilliant, really something.

CHAPTER EIGHT

The Bush Era

THE NEXT TIME YOU WOULD BE WITH HER was almost as awkward, after so much IM, e-mail and web page exchanges. After so many hours jerking off to the never-ending supply of photos. She took photographs of herself constantly, everywhere. Was it a kind of autoeroticism, or sexual sublimation? Still, it was a happy reunion. Because she was Alistair's classmate, Charlie found it difficult to come around. She was fond of the boy, although she described him as both sad and a keener.

Being such a keener, he had occasion to organize and promote extracurricular school activities. It made your eyes roll, politely, in that it was at least a silent complaint.

Charlie made her way up to your study during act something, scene something of Shakespeare's something or other.
She stood in the doorway while you sat, busying yourself
with forceful longing. She came to you—which was best,
because you couldn't get up. She sat on your lap and poured
a drink for each of you. You relaxed, felt looser. Your throat
was still tight, so you just drank without talking, far too aware
of her ass on your crotch, wondering if it was damp—the
fabric between you. You put your hand down the front of
her skirt. It was very much as it had been in your adoles-
cence—there wasn't a clear understanding of what you were
allowed to do. Her pussy was smooth, probably shaved. The
young girl thing to do, apparently. She must have noticed
your noticing. She said, "Did you expect something else?"

Was the kid trying to embarrass you?

"A big seventies bush? Is that what your girlfriends
have?" She thought she was being very funny, waiting for
the laugh riot.

"I don't have girlfriends. No. Not at all."

"I can grow a bush. I had one until I was thirteen. Is it a
sign of virtue for men your age?"

"God no. It's not. You're really very mouthy in person."

"I'm just having fun. Aren't we having fun?"

Of course you were. You were having the best night of
your life.

It was difficult to continue; she'd broken your concentration, your hard-on was losing its character, things were just
not right. The position you were in, in the chair—it was solid

wood, a beautiful Sam Spade kind of thing built for grown men of business—wasn't made for fooling around. But the panties and the stockings? They were doing a fine job. So you drank more, smoked cigarettes and talked. You wouldn't be her first time; at twelve some lucky hockey player had enjoyed that honour—a botched threesome between her best friend and her best friend's sister's husband. The other girl pussied out and left Charlie to her own devices: bland and mercifully short-lived factory-town fucking. She told you it was okay but not anything unique, and that "He left his hat on, which was a good focal point."

Not being her first was A-okay with you.

CHAPTER NINE

Health Punt

A GIRL DOESN'T MAKE YOU INTO A MAN, surely, but her presence, the thought of her, made you want to become a man again. Charlie was a catalyst. Nadine couldn't do this; Nadine's wiles were diluted by an onslaught of pseudo-feministas in couture-fitted yoga wear. After Nicola, your second daughter, was born, you put out for a mom-job—the tummy tuck was all Nadine was after, but you were trying to be generous. A fine surgeon, recoup time, live-out nanny (you had your limits). Nadine had always had a great body, a killer ass as more than one of your friends had pronounced it, and good, even better than good, tits. But after the babies and the mothering, things had changed, dropped. You still noticed other men looking at her, leaning in to talk to her at parties, holding her hand a little too long after a handshake—their standards, it stood to reason, were lower; they didn't know she'd been even better, before. Nadine was lively and energetic, she was, you remembered, a skillful young mother and housewife and she made it work, painlessly, each day, a magic trick none of your friends' gals had ever been able to match.

You felt guilty about the fling you had with Barbara, Peter's wife. Barbara the Lush. She talked about Nadine while she showered, as she dressed. She smelled like (not of) dirty martinis, new car and menthol. It was the eighties after all; the affair lasted only a couple of months. But she'd gone slightly rabid when you broke it off. You might have been worried, but she seemed too drunk to properly compile her facts and present them to the involved parties. Barbara was not a careful woman and she served as an *aide-mémoire* about the importance of a healthy, happy wife—a good mother, a well-kept lady of the house.

Times changed. Nadine had changed—you hadn't. Men like you were not built this way; you had only limited options, and they never involved vegetarianism or retreats. The options were work/sex/money/leisure (the leather club-chair, tanned-and-boozy version of leisure). But things changed, yes, and maybe you *were* a little different—maybe you had been misled, conned; maybe you too were young and dynamic and happy, even healthy? Charlie, the catalyst, the cataclysm—the jewel in the crown of your miserably lucky existence. Maybe you were—was it possible—in love?

Nadine was sharp, intellectual, and you would never say anything to the contrary or listen to any similar kind of slander from any woman since Barbara the Talking Bush. But Nadine had been conditioned, primed by the order of daytime television personalities. She decided against surgery and used the money you had given her to fund a macrobiotic/spiritual/holistic/earth-mother rip-off. These women were cruel and manipulative, as only women—let us be frank—can be. They stole Nadine's contented psyche. You may be thinking that's what Tolstoy said seven years before the revolt, the revolution. But Jules would say, maybe the peasants were happy. (What a dick you might say here.) Maybe seven years later the world wasn't so enamoured with its happy peasants and so they were, by necessity, different people. This was the proviso, the clause built into our future. It was unfair and a dirty trick at best, but you were not cool anymore. And as for Tolstoy's masses, their mirror was telling them different things too. And, as you know, things changed. The world told Nadine she wasn't doing enough, that her years of study and travel were inconsequential after years of mothering and wife-ing. Mutually exclusive, these awful women convinced her. "Do more," they admonished, "because you can"—a mantra eerily similar to the "be-more TV icon" your girls talked about on the phone after class each day. The purpose of this show, the sovereign monarchy of modern womanhood, was vague—guests brandished delightful stories of being pummelled to the perimeter of life; how they single-manicured-handedly wrestled their way back, made crazy money, wrote a book. . . . And then the close-up and the cry, a formula not unlike the porn of days gone by: the money shot the first discharge of tears; the post-lick the couch hug.

Things would change again; darkness emptied into darkness no more. Your night light, your full-up pipe in a cold-cracked apartment—our girl Charlie, she inspired you. You would become a man. It would take some doing and some undoing but just looking at her bruised knees, a pictogram of the newly random universe she was letting you into, was enough to get you started, to get you fit.

CHAPTER TEN

Like Bridges, Burning

THAT IT IS NOT OKAY TO KEEP YOURSELF CAGED UP in your office all day was the feeling you'd gotten from Nadine and, occasionally, one of the presumptuous and bluntly out-of-line children. When the door was forced open you didn't bolt up, as you often imagined you would have to were such a thing to ever happen. The door was, in reality, heavy and took a moment to open, longer than they expected. You had calculated everything, knew the response time of every floorboard and bedspring and hinge in the house—and still you didn't respond as predicted. No one expects you to sit in your office and remember shit all day, Jules. Not your family and not the reader. But no one with a heart would want to make you jump, a man in your state—oldish, hot, tired and in the throes of an impressive existential failure. The realizing, the change-making stuff. Religion, or in your case, the time-consuming consumption: narrow size six white tennis shoes for her, health food shops, omega oils, co-Q 10, Botox and cotton candy number thirty-six nail gloss. Nothing expensive really, just constant enough to be consistent, the thing any observer would conclude was that thing that kept you alive.

You had always believed that constant movement—working, sailing, fucking, drinking, driving—could occupy you to distraction. This is you, your one life. (Unless you believe the one or so billion people in hot, dry countries that believe otherwise—tell me you don't.)

And this is it?

You never answered. You just kept moving, aimlessly forward. There would never come a time when you could stop. That's the way it was. The more days you spent in bed with Charlie, reading week-old papers, smoking cigarettes and little else, the less you moved, the harder it became to go back. What if you had to go back? Charlie was of the opinion that progress and achievement made us grow and age and die, while painting your nails and sleeping and reading and failing and falling in love were the forces that kept all the nasty parts of life somewhere out of sight. But Charlie could be young and thoughtless. She had lived very few years and all of those as Charlie. You'd lived as this guy, this dick. You advised, made deals, called people, had very little loyalty and never spent a moment thinking about it—that wasn't what guys like you did. Every day, with the exception of a few, was just nothing. A few. A few days away from our girl amounted to memories or memories digested and reproduced in photographic image. You had suspicions that in the end it would all become clear: that a day spent sitting in your office doing fuck-all would be no more or less momentous at seventy-one or whatever your body decided was the last straw (stuck through a cherry in some girl's drink), than a day jumping out of a plane with a parachute that almost didn't open. If your life could write its own epitaph you imagined it might say: *It hardly mattered.*

So yeah, you had spent too long by yourself in there and, yes, they did push the door open to surprise you.

Surprise.

And yes, this is how they found you: crying on the floor, your robe open, and Charlie's girl-space photos on your computer screen.

What was it, a couple of party guests? That seemed right. Nadine.

You looked up, but you didn't jump. That wasn't a guy like you thing to do your body must've decided. The air around became so . . . altered. It smelled like bridges, burning.

In late June of 1990-something a bunch of people walked in and saw you crying, holding (cradling?) your cock like it were a dead baby in front of a number of gorgeous and wholly inappropriate images of a fifteen-year-old girl.

You thought about the numbers; everything became quantitative. Reasoning would get you through this crisis; numbers would protect you. You'd made a pact with them in 1975 when you gave up living as a human and became a businessman. The numbers owed you.

CHAPTER ELEVEN

Dead Ringer

IN A DRAWER INSIDE THE BAR (hidden in your deco desk) are things of value: a slim fireproof safe, a suicide note, a copy of your will and a ring you couldn't afford in your dirty thirties when your wife had seen it in a Cartier window display. The ring was (of course) an easy decision. At roughly twenty-nine thousand bones it might be the grenade you needed to escape this fortress of relentless familiarity—out of the light and into the deep blue, bruised legs of your true love. Fuck, and fuck, you should have said. But instead, a calm—a cool trick of the psyche—pulled your shit together and you went outside.

All the usual Sashas and Katerinas and Davids and whatshernames were there. You walked out and waited for locusts; it was too late for the first-born. You fingered the ring in your pocket, tongued an apologetic greeting, an excuse extraordinaire. And nothing at all like this happened. Something worse happened: nothing at all. Nadine smiled and patted your shoulder and one of your pals' wives who was in the scandal suite a few moments earlier shook your hand—the one that had been holding your bag. Was she fucking oblivious?

When you finally corner Nadine she's smiling—not with thin lips, more of an empathy thing.

"It's okay, Jules. It's okay, all right? Nobody cares."

You definitely heard "Nobody cares."

Her hand rested on your shoulder for just a moment and yet you felt it there forever(ish), for the rest of the party at least. Like the easy tone of a teenager on an answering machine the night he wraps his shitbox around a telephone post, some things are most alarming in their kind and familiar form. "Nobody cares" would be, you decided, a couple of words that would assist you in disappearing, unabashedly, deeper into your random disorder of anxiety, insomnia, infidelity and pills.

It's okay. Nobody cares.

What does this mean?

You didn't ask; Nadine was gone. The disappearing act

was her *magnum opus*. The magnetic woman, people orbiting her—but there was no room for you.

There's knowing and *knowing*, as you know. If a woman *knew* she could mess you up—your friends, family, every asshole you worked with, your files and clients—nothing could ever be safe and sound. She could write about it, were she the type; she'd call your mother, if she were alive. . . . In layman Jules-speak: she'd fuck your shit up.

But sometimes a girl knew—an unclear idiom that kept your balls safely sacked, if only provisionally. A girl knew things weren't right, and you weren't right. That was something different entirely.

What Nadine knew paid for a two-month first-class family vacation to the U.K. It picked up the bill for day trips outside of the secure, rented London-yuppie flat (quite beyond what your Rosedale digs could fetch, even with top-end maid form) to Leeds, the dirty, seedy Ottawa of Britain, as you came to see it. You were reconnecting with your family, and with Nadine and her family, who thought you to be a cock and dismissed your company lock, stock and barrel: a fact that both suited you well and freed up some time.

CHAPTER TWELVE

—

Angel and the Hired Hand

AT 10:30-ISH—HARD TO BELIEVE, I KNOW—Nadine's relatives and the rest of your family were turning in, turning down and turning out (the lights). The home? A filthy-posh five-bedroom Georgianesque reno. All the discomforts: plush white carpeting, art nouveau décor and black-lacquer-and-ivory kitchen casings. It was unusually visible from the street, hidden poorly behind a sterile Japanese garden and two older model Porsches—not classic and gauche in their late-eighties colour schemes. A complex, no, cruel, punch-button alarm system would have tripped you up, but for your lifelong affair with numbers. The side entrance was the better way to break out. The 21 bus? Nope. A taxi. What's money for, after all, if not the perfect getaway? A compact wet Beamer—windows wound tight, heated and hot-boxed, coerced through the roundabout and twenty-odd downtown turns by Les, a half-tanked and violently cheerful sixty-year-old who asked you for directions at least twice—in between life lessons, investment advice (how shit hair cost you in the long run and made people think you were a right prat), the difference between a mate and a "fucking ponce," and the boisterous airing of the dirtiest of family linens.

Les was a good guy.

And, it was worth it. You had once spent your last tenner (in Les-speak) on a cab; cigarettes and taxis kept and created continuity and, unlike work and women, didn't offer immediate dissension. By midnight you were in Heaven. Across the street was Hell—a weak stab at a dungeon, a sad attempt at a sad trend: sex so boring it needed to be accessorized with impractical straps and chains. The whole thing reeked of D&D "outsider" affectation, but tapped into the isolated sex-offender-to-be market. Naturally, the place was packed. And you were in Heaven, in Angel—cute as a kitten and collecting for methamphetamine debts and rent via your dick with all pink-coloured and time-honored orifices in play. Angel, the name each young lady gave herself in Heaven, though you never asked, before you bent her over the spick-and-span but bitter, cold-as-a-post-communist-Bucharest-orphan's-heart marble bathroom counter. You fell into shop talk with Nadine's nephew Leo.

Leo was one of the few from your extended family (any family, if you were to be honest) you could relate to. And right now that relating was nothing less than insufferable. He had debts. Gambling. Proper money, proper losses, as he put it. None of that online casino wanker and housemaid action—a real bookie who broke real fingers with a real crowbar. At least he paid someone to do it. So, while you should be in heaven, over the moon, you aren't because Leo is an aggravating white noise. And, well, because you are in love, and love makes you sick and socially retarded. It happens to us all, for a while. Your main concern was Charlie meeting almost anyone else and running off. You didn't have the guts to ask, "What do they have that I don't," because you were afraid of the answer. Things like better looking, less-married and kidded-up, more mature, adventurous, and happy all sprang to mind.

You had to get back.

"Leo, I have to get back. Can you get me back?" You wiped your Angel clean of your own attempt at accessorizing hell, the imprecise cum-shot on any old (but undeniably young) faultless back.

He could, Leo said. He could do anything you were after. Except "off" someone—that was not his racket.

In the morning, or the afternoon of sober adult time, you made your way freely—with gracious waves bye-bye from the family—to the David David club. Fitness classes, yoga studio, juice bar, co-ed saunas and a credible lounge and wet bar. Men and women smoking like it was keeping them fit and drinking reasonably stiff cocktails (unlike the pop-and-candy concoctions every kid downed their pills and rails with in the nightclubs of this city). Neat and tidy with nothing else, or nothing but ice or soda, thank Christ. Charlie had learned to drink Scotch, as stubborn as she was. You'd convinced her that it was better and more romantic than the gin and diet tonics you couldn't stomach (or liver) after the wooing stage had ended. Had she moved on; had she got your letter? Did she fondly remember the early fondling and arguments? The break-in, the breakfast at three in the three-day weekend at the Royal York when neither of you left the room? Maybe she didn't care to remember—in which case, what a bitch. Could it be that she had not cared the whole time?

Leo ordered two doubles. You corrected him but he insisted. "You'll need a double mate, all right? Two doubles and a single, love." A large man came in, a cop or criminal—it was impossible to tell, both types looked around far too quickly, checking exits, adjusting blazers and mouths. Who else would they be here for? And yet they didn't seem to recognize him. "Leo?" they leaned in politely so as not to disturb the other smokers from their bleeding heart-to-hearts. "Sorry. Mickey gave me forty quid for this, pal." He said "pal" with a stutter that was very difficult not to empathize with.

Then, out came the crowbar. A fucking crowbar! What was this, Manchester, 1975? Bradford, right now? You felt your bladder's warm aspirations, but you tensed up in time. Vomit?

No, hold it together. Pppppthal. Don't interfere. Leo is a good guy and all, but this is his business. Forty pounds, etc. Don't lose it. Don't piss yourself.

And then, Leo nodded. Flinched? Nope, as confusing as it was, it was most assuredly a nod, sideways. What the fuck? And then your right hand was broken; Leo's fingers were broken. He'd been careful enough, you found out later. He'd been an okay guy about it, apologizing and patting Leo's back afterwards.

Was nobody outraged? No, they were not. They kept lighting and pulling and clinking, swirling ice and laughing. It was the laughter that made you vomit and the vomit that made "Love," the waitress, throw you out. "Go on outside now, love." So hard to be pissed at a girl like that—manners and all.

Leo had made good on his promise. Like the reprobate he was. It took a sociopath to get you home with the respect and sympathy of Nadine's relatives. You threw down some extra cash for an early flight. That wasn't, thankfully, "what the whole family ought to do." And you returned to your wonderfully empty three-level house, deep behind the maple trees, the garden, the driveway and the curtains and the walls and walls and walls. You returned to your office, to your dear laptop in your lonely heart-attack suite.

CHAPTER THIRTEEN

Yellow Brick, Goodbye

HOME WAS MOST ASSUREDLY SWEET. Bern sat nonchalantly in the garden. The bed was fresh and the phone did not ring incessantly. Nobody knew you were here—nobody cared. Your hand was shit but well wrapped with much unwanted attention by a busty nurse tipping the scales at, let's say, two-fifty. Nothing wrong with that; just not your thing. A niche fuck. Your preferences are vague and varied but did not include overt come-ons, bright-light television makeup or perfumes. It didn't include women whose only strong suit was cleavage, at least not for anything past a two-night stand.

Home was sweetened by the echo of empty halls—but there were still problems, right?

Insomnia. Like many of your problems: untreatable. You never took your useful meds; they worried you, even though you'd, on occasion, down handfuls of unnamed pills from beautiful glossy little bags on girls' nightstands. You weren't sleeping. You were waiting. Waiting was a verb, a foul little secret, your laptop volume dial turned up to a level that made anything that wasn't what you wanted so mind-shatteringly annoying, each IM ding would take minutes off your already short life.

You saved your history with Charlie, knowing no one else ever opened this laptop. In fact, it was almost always with you—as close as possible at any rate. The messages and photos were a reprieve from the heartache, the gut-rot. Where are you, my girl? Doing bumps off bank cards in some business-casual's Merc? In bed, dreaming horrible little girl dreams? Tied up and gagged in a Yonge-and-Steeles basement?

What happened to our girl?

You'd never asked before now. Love had gone off beam and was, in its every molecule, barbed and twisted in your memory into loathing and a bottomless self-pity. This'd be how a guy ended up breaking a girl's neck, or stabbing her twenty-seven times (hesitation wounds excluded), or just laying on the floor of an empty two-point-five-million-dollar home. (The latter option requiring a little less from you in the way of physical exertion.) You called the housekeeper and told her to fuck off for the week (with pay), an act that required the raw power of all of your faculties operating at full force. This created more time for laying around on the immaculate hardwood, listening to Elton John albums, and weeping—that was the only word for it—becoming younger, better-looking the less you ate, and more determined and more deranged the less you slept. This was your renaissance, you told yourself as you unfolded, light into more light, and you were screwing it up. A physical impossibility, like water to wine, our girl Charlie, not even sweet sixteen, ward of the state, misappropriated-refugee-allowance-benefactor and the best thing to happen to you since the Mulroney-Regan Alliance with its celebrated channelling of Free Trade cash which you would never admit to under any oath. She had brought you to your knees, and if only briefly, raised you from vagueness and ambiguity into preciseness, authenticity, back to yourself or whoever it was you were supposed to become after you were grunted into existence. It had happened, was happening—and now, static, nothingness and painkillers.

When the single malt ran out, you crawled on hands and knees in a more determined manner to the library. Searching in drawers and then beneath, behind books, up the staircase. The stairs took time, but your need was great and required such stick-to-it-iveness. Pills, they answered questions. Booze only asked why, how did this happen and do you love me? Pills replied with a pretty smile, a glossy kiss, a powdery happy softness. The wonderful muted fear, the knowledge, the anxiety and starvation and slaughter just far enough from the perverse, an itch at most. That was the chemical. They answered; yes, they answered, it's okay; and something that sounded like "I love you" too.

Your older daughter, Beth—the one you thought of as the fat one, though she hadn't been fat for five years—had only bennies, jennies, laxatives and diuretics which were of no help. The stuff Nadine usually swept for—maybe she had missed the obvious sock rolls and sanitary pad boxes. But she wasn't one of you, was she? Thank fuck for scrips. You closed your eyes and picked the left hand, took a few of those. Anything red, pink, white or blue was in play. Dying was about the only thing of importance you could get around to doing this afternoon. Goodbye little darlings. And you heard their sweet goodbye. It may have been Elton, but let's agree that someone, somewhere, answered. That no one was asking, and that's all you cared about.

If you live through this, looking up now at the yellow Devonshire cream walls, you think about Nadine's friend June considering, aloud, that maybe exposed brick was "over." You let it go. After all she had electric-ish boots, a mohair-ish suit. . . . Like everything once considered cool, it no longer was, and you hadn't renovated in a forever and ever sense, had not foreseen the end of the era. But something needed to be done about the walls, if you did in fact wake up: a phone call, a can of paint, whatever.

CHAPTER FOURTEEN

All the Young Dudes

LIKE THE '68 COMEBACK SPECIAL, you were neither coming back nor was there anything particularly special about you. You surveyed the room, looked up at the glow of the television—Princess Di's wedding, her suitors, smash-ups, some Jackie O and her new man footage, the aftermath, their descendants, that type of deal. Who were these new men? *Other* men. They were better looking than you, way better: younger looking by decades. Times were changing; you weren't. You were still kind of fat, and death was coming for you like gangbusters. Still, it was years off, and that was all right.

You were, after all, the sleep-it-off king. As such, this late morning was going swimmingly.

You were alive. And that wasn't as bad as it might seem to the people who knew you. You didn't look half-bad after a night's sleep. Passing the mirror you stopped—you'd be enough to keep a girl's feet under the table, or her shoes under the bed for the night at least. You *had* made a few calls in haste, completely easy and not at all embarrassing with the aid of blue pill and white tablet. You'd dialed numbers from Alistair's cell phone, left behind because it wouldn't charge abroad. A broad was what you were looking for, a small one who wore a tuxedo T-shirt and silver tights or nothing at all. Or knee socks, or rubber boots and a hairpin and nothing else.

There were rumours she'd been shacking up with someone young-ish in the west end. There were a few she'd been around and another possible guy downtown; and of course, some said she was with someone older. Had to be you, right? It's not okay to steal a guy's girl, even if you were her age, roughly, and she dropped by your place willingly. You'd done it a few times and made your peace with that. It was one of the universal immoral facts; most men of your era, epoch, could agree upon this. When it happened to you it was up to other guys or knockout women to say don't think twice: I hated her; don't think about her; so many shining little fish in the sea; what a slut she was. It didn't have to be true; it was never true. You did think twice.

You did think twice and it wasn't all right. You thought a million times and the velocity of this cycle only became more exhausting. Being you, sitting there doing nothing at all, was becoming gruelling.

When you finally found the key to Charlie's place, under the potted plants on her stoop, you thought about opening the door and remembered the "crime of passion" trials you'd advised on. What dreary, drawn-out affairs they always were. You never came here, pardoning your own pun. It wasn't risky, it was just ridiculously stupid. The daylight was broad enough that you could be seen, and as much as you tell yourself that Italian designer sunglasses block out the death wish of neighbour and foe, it was a bad time to show up unannounced at the home of a minor you wanted to murder or fuck, or both. But an amateur magician acting like a dick across the street would probably attract more attention. He was smashing his car window with a planter, which was also smashed. "Tactical ventilation!" he yelled, taking the heat off you and laughing as though it were not even a mildly embarrassing thing for a seventy-year-old man in a bathrobe to be doing. The side of his car read *The Magnificent Rinaldo*. You nodded and ducked your head into your collar for cover.

The house felt mod bobo—almost always an indication of privilege gone wrong. Inside were a couple of guys cutting white shit with other white stuff. It looked responsible enough, baking soda and not cleansers or other home remedies. Cutting clean narcotics with dirty yellowing agents was the young thug's best shot at ready money. These boys were suburban and heartless but wouldn't be up on charges of negligent homicide anytime soon. Nobody thought it strange that you were walking through the pink-on-pink kitchen of the kid's semi-detached. You were effectively invisible. It may have been the glasses; yeah, that was possible. You walked at a leisurely pace through a bright hallway labelled *Warhall* (you wanted to murder the prep-school fuck who did this). Girls' faces were staggered down the length of it, and at the end you found four of Charlie. You recognized her in the negative. You kept walking and stumbled right through the fourth wall. The wall that you had so loved—you had entered into its "legal" minor monarchy, agreeing to and abiding by the terms of its contract: that it was there to protect you from your own reality. This was clear in the small print beneath your credit card number and expiry date as you signed in with the burden of the 3 a.m. hard-on. What the fuck, you might have said. But you didn't. You spoke through the wall, from stage left:

"Honey?"

As though that was her given name. But then your screen name was Rinaldo because you were professional and married, so who knew, right?

"Busy, hun."

She continued masturbating robotically, aimed toward the web cam beneath the security camera and to the right of *The Young and the Restless* playing on the LCD monitor hung on the wall. Stucco everywhere, like it was a Mediterranean villa, or more accurately, a tiny and equally sex-fuelled Tel Aviv Bauhaus-style bedroom, all stuccoed white-on-white walls and linens and silk sheets. You thought more intensely about this until a surprisingly painful sensation gave you cause to hold your nutsack in plain view yet again.

"Get the fuck out of here you perverted old pedo."

That was roughly how the whole thing went down. This young dude throwing you out, cold-speak like a scorned woman. You wanted to ask, "Christ, did you have to say old? And perverted?" But not fat, that at least was a civilized touch. Those were unkind terms, hard or at least tricky to stomach; words that would require more pills; your balls, on the other hand, were soft and would need booze and ice, in any order.

Back on your floor things were more forgiving. You should have been (but weren't even close to being) ashamed of yourself when you got back to find her there, after your madman P.I. search. Charlie was waiting for you like a little angel, her hair cut with a mother's stroke—it looked cheap and youthful. Parted straight as an arrow.

"I missed you," you may have said, and she definitely must have said, "Where've you been?" "Around." Were those part of your reunion? Yeah, they were important to you as well. What you are clear on was that you smoked your way through a carton of American cigarettes together and talked about things of no consequence. Was she back?

"Are you back?"

"I am," one of you probably said.

CHAPTER FIFTEEN

Good Morning
(Little Schoolgirl)

IT IS CLEAR ENOUGH; most guys don't want a good thing for another guy. And even clearer, let's say doubly true, that girls don't want a good thing to happen to another girl—especially if she is even slightly more beautiful and her tits stand even insignificantly higher. So at this point some of you may be inclined to want something bad to happen to our girl, or better still, our main man—as though this was all just about moral order. Decent stand-up citizens know love speaks the language of vagabonds and thieves. But, the narrator might suggest here, if you speak this language too, the exchange may not be so difficult. Charlie and Jules had been speaking the language fluently, thick as felons, at ease with depravity, and it had gotten them nowhere, or at least not to where they wanted to be most, back to their beginnings, to the study, the very secure room. Decadence is always bad for a guy's health. Your analyst, spiritual Sherpa, drug dealer, faith healer and cab driver have told you this many times: decadence was heavy, sticky and corrupted. Asceticism, that popular form of denial you tried to sell yourself time and again, wasn't sticking. Maybe they were all wrong. Was it possible? Apparently. It seemed as though they had never woken naked, bourgeois-casual, in the arms (or between the thighs) of a young girl, then just gone back to sleep in an empty bastard of a home, without reprisal.

If you had forgotten anything about teenage sex, you were about to be reacquainted with its wonder. Remembering you hadn't had full-on whole-hog sex with a fifteen-year-old since you were fourteen, blow jobs and fingering had kept you blue-balling your way through frustrating nights of repression and common sleeplessness for months.

It was what you'd expect: sickeningly perfect and abstract fucking, panties to the side, biting, hitting and laughing in the face of what should have been looming and staggering consequences.

Later on you would talk about the apartment situation—you didn't, of course, approve of the drugs and pornography. Charlie admitted to nothing except for a photo spread in *Naughty Next Door* which she later included in a birthday card, a darling centerfold, wallet-sized, fitting perfectly behind your American Express card. A schoolgirl motif, the classic magazine porn shot, though it was typically carried out inaccurately, featuring a tanned-up thirty-year-old model whose gaping lower orifices you could shoot craps in. It wasn't a stretch, Charlie said, fifteen at the shoot, to play the role of eighteen-year-old Annabelle Cherry of 234 Morning Glory Circle whose interests included babysitting and gymnastics. But no, there would definitely be no internet porn or drug industry guys you didn't know about, she promised. That said, you didn't feel good about where she was at. You'd get Charlie her very own quarters in the annex where she'd blend in a bit and be close by, if she liked the arrangement. She did, of course; she thought it was wonderful. You let these bits of affected affection go because they really were awfully charming.

The two of you began to have a good time—properly. You went out openly, shopping, looking at apartments and drinking in hotel bars and hole-in-the-wall dives. Sometimes you would be needed, something would come up at work, a sex scandal involving three members of the law firm you associated with as clients number nine, seventeen and twenty-one, and as such you were needed in the office a little more. Aside from these instances of momentary real-life acquaintanceship you both managed your affair like it was the right thing to be doing. You relaxed and had brazen moments of happiness not always related to levels of toxicity or hormonal freedom and sexual release. You smiled a lot more. Neither of you were thinking about the twelve alcohol-fuelled dark days suffered by families in the northern blackout, the three charred babies of California's wildfires, the seven kids shot down during math class in the high school not so far from Charlie's new apartment, or the however-many starving children of Africa. (They were still starving, you assumed.) You weren't that kind of guy right now and she wasn't that kind of girl. You were shooting off blanks from antique revolvers in separate bedrooms, working your way through your pill stockpile and drinking from the bottle (bottle after bottle). Charlie wore eighteen pieces of candy jewelry to an art opening in the distillery district, which for some reason, or none at all, seemed to piss off the older set, the once-were-attractives who blew smoke out of their nostrils and applied lipstick persistently. You went out to a burlesque club and dined with Peter, who was desperately trying to act laid back in his stiff academic glad rags, and spent the entire evening trying to embezzle some affection from your girl, before finally tiring at about two. Neither of you seemed to notice or mind. You drank Tiki drinks from coconuts on the porch of a hostile working-class neighbourhood house party and woke up drunk in someone's backyard. Things were going well. And when Nadine and the rest of the family returned, you hadn't thought to greet their homecoming in any special way. You hadn't thought of them at all.

CHAPTER SIXTEEN

Reaganomics

IN AUGUST OF 1985 NADINE'S FATHER GARY BECAME ILL. His cancer had spread from lung to everywhere. To say he was pissed off would be both accurate and an understatement. He had been your go-to guy, intelligent, difficult, sophisticated and very good with people. You feared and respected him (while not agreeing with him on many issues), and quite possibly loved him—as young men sometimes do when an older, far greater man backs them. He did his best with the macabre death scenes, rolling his new wheelchair to the end of the dock without the physical capacity to get over the edge, falling on a knife and finally, and frequently, ordering you all to kill him. Gary was always fucking great at persuading people, especially ladies, to see his point. Before Nadine, with the backing of her sisters and brothers, stabbed him with a needle full of lethal morphine (which was hard for you to resist dipping into at that time) Gary said a few goodbyes and as a final point, left you all with the question, the grand *au revoir.* "Why does Reagan get to live when I have to die?"

Whether this stuck with you because it was the final question from one of your very few real friends, because it was truly one the best days in your marriage or because it made you laugh wasn't clear. But it did; it stuck. It was sticking like a rusty needle today—not life-ending stuff, but enough to make a man want to cry.

Bern is dying was the look Nadine gave you. Fuck her. Did you mean that? Nothing was comprehensible. She was great with real life, adult life. She was good with blood and guts and phone calls, leaking faucets, taxes, adolescent "issues" and pulling the trigger, or the plug, opposite actions with equally fatal consequences. The shotgun approach seemed far less cruel, to go out in a hail of buckshot, blood and screaming; it was the physical representation, the full-colour response to the event that was taking place inside, the brutal and messy adieu. Was it fair to pull a plug, empty a vial? It was the sedentary desk-bound Mister Nobody goodbye: the big fuck you.

"What should we do?" You were surprised by your own voice. But speaking seemed the far better option, if quietly speculating on how to say something was at all unhealthy for your souring ulcer-prone gut.

"I don't know yet. Wait, I'd say." Nadine was thinking, loosening Bern's collar.

"Take it off."

"Yeah, I suppose, it just seems strange." Nadine was hesitating and taking her time the way we do when we are doing anything at all for the last time. She was a person who cared about this kind of thing, she would wear Richard's wedding ring, moving it down the line of fingers, from the left hand to the right, year after year, until one year it disappeared, you didn't ask where. Likewise she couldn't stand to look at the auto dealership that had your first family car for sale on its lawn, after the ends finally met and you could upgrade to an Alfa Romeo. (What a machine. Weren't you the man in those days?) And, because it was Bern, you appreciated the time it took to get the collar off.

"He'll be more comfortable," someone said. And on you went with this kind of small talk, frozen in your furious grief.

There was an hour or two of this and then Nadine decided to drag the turntable and a stack of LPs into the room and you convinced her to smoke cigarettes, a marital *coup d'état* which now allowed you to chain smoke with impunity.

It wasn't a sexual thing, lying on the floor (with the dog

dying between you), smoking, changing the album when you remembered a better one. It wasn't sexual; it was life during wartime. Everything of value is eventually hunted down and stolen or killed. This was the great truth of the human experience. Bern was lucky, what you had thought of as a flaw in the evolutionary process was, as revealed to you now, a fortunate failure in acquiring the biological rights to access consciousness: the unparalleled buffer. You reached in your pocket and found your own luck, offered Nadine her own Lorazapam, which she took, with a "Christ" or "Give it here." Either way you both relaxed a bit and benefited from the flattering special effects of twilight—when everyone looks better.

CHAPTER SEVENTEEN

Death Blow

IT WASN'T SEXUAL: this was your wife, your home, your dying
dog. But as I said, the lighting, the night. . . . Death—that
maudlin slut—she got you every time. All the fear and
anxiety and mother seeking—you always went to Nadine in
these times. It'd just been a while, and so you rolled over
Bern and lay on her stomach.

"You have great tits."

"You're stoned, Jules."

She wasn't annoyed, just maybe overtaxed, almost amused,
brushing your hair back like she did with Alistair.

"I'm the same as always. I'm just commenting on your

rack, which is nearly perfect, is all." It didn't need poetic shit directed at it either, it was the real deal and you said so.

"What's wrong, Jules?"

"This whole thing." You swallowed an oxy for your hand with the help of Nadine's bottle of wine. "It's bullshit. Bern? That's not going to be easy to live with. But everything else. . . . Everything. Is this how you wanted everything to be?"

"I don't know. No, probably not. I guess. You know I wanted to be a mother and to have a house and a yard and friends and a dog. Is that what you're asking?"

"Mmm-hmm."

"What did you want?" Nadine had a way of laughing that was kind and surprising and sometimes made you feel like a self-indulgent dick.

"I don't know. Something different. Not really better, just something else." With this, the chemicals, ebbing toward blood-poisoning, were launching a malfunction in your genitals and sending you to sleep. If you had told Nadine you loved her and made a play for her breasts it would have been half booze, twenty-five percent narcotic and a few parts male vehemence and legitimate sentiment. In any case it was the first time you'd lay down to sleep beside your wife in a few years. If she had let you have a brief go at her bra, it was her own *coup de grâce*, the final hit you needed before sleep.

The benefits of your opulent Victorian renovation were many: the remarkable amount of unnecessary space, for example, allowed for endless privacy. The shutters, draperies, doors and your penchant for soundproofing materials also made it easy to skulk and sneak up on people—even when you weren't trying to, when you were just going for cereal. It was especially easy to surprise half-sober middle-aged people.

At 9 a.m. your daughters and son were already looking down at you.

"Mom?"

They seemed frightened, shaken. You seemed to feel like you should be feeling guilty, ashamed. They seemed to believe in some perverse "goodness," as though you should have turned into a eunuch after their births. Children are the absolute, unsurpassed royalty of the self-righteous kingdom.

"What's going on? Why are you in here?"

It was the first time they'd seen the two of you together in the morning for . . . maybe forever. Rigor settling into Bern, dead soldiers lining the vacant stone fireplace, ashtrays overflowing on the dado rails. Albums, a beautifully crumpled Harry Rosen jacket and slacks, pill bottles and your good hand down the front of your boxers—all of these things may have contributed to the disgust and pity directed at you from above.

Nadine didn't seem to feel the same way; she was tough and wonderful with the offspring. "We're trying to sleep. . . . The dog's dead." Maybe she was just extremely hungover. Either way it sweetened her pot—any girl who let a guy have a lie-in was worth her weight in clean bills.

CHAPTER EIGHTEEN

The Other Half

YOU HAD OUTLIVED YOUR DOG and the "inevitable" break-down of your marriage—was that possible? Outliving your filthy go at reductionism: finding those little parts that make up deteriorating manhood and milking the hell out of them. You should be in the late stages of a mid-life fuck-up, a mass exodus (separation, divorce and its expensive, cliché trappings, hot and dangerous places, girls and cars). But, as luck would have it, you had been living with the symptoms of this wonderful, bountiful illness all your adult life. It seemed a shame to go into remission just as a full-blown excuse for it all appeared, a cure for your ailing reputation. But what could you do? You'd spent the night with your wife and it was good—better than it should've been.

You don't ask yourself, is she real? Is this her? Do I love her? That's not the kind of thing a guy asks about his wife— a guy can roll over and pinch his wife anytime he wants to, she's liable to be there most of the time. She wasn't there though. You pinched the trillion thread-count pillow casing instead. It'd been a while since you'd had the occasion (or desire) to touch your wife and you were still approximately half-tanked. Maybe she did a lot on weekends? It was possible, everything was kept so clean and orderly—it had to be, in some way, partly Nadine's doing, right? She sure as hell had been busy in the bedroom—a stack and sprawl of classics on her bedside table, dog-eared and ringed with what smelled faintly like some kind of gypsy caravan tea.

"Nadine!" You called for her from under the duvet, one eye slightly but intensely open, as though it would help in eliciting a response.

"I'm dying. Nadine? Nadine! Can you send some water up? Water. Nadiiiiiine."

And you fell back asleep in the midst of a dehydration crisis, thanks to a first-rate, solid Deboers bed and half a Stella (then the other half).

It wasn't that type of sickening life-altering love-lust. It wasn't like Charlie—this was your wife. No, it was more the "everything is all right" variety soft-news item, the quasi-passion, the status quo—a little respite of order and substance amid the anarchic gale out to get you. It was agony at times, this longstanding guilt. Handling your discretion with indiscretions—that too was wearing. It was also good and saved your ass more than once. It could also be a safe place, a safe bet, better known as your marriage, or Jules and Nadine to foreigners and friends. And it made them feel all right, too. Hangover energy was your stand-in for general wellbeing, but it bottomed out in eight hours. Best to strike while the alcohol was still metabolizing and take two anti-anxieties to help outrun the darkness de jour trying to catch up with you. They helped a lot with any psychological state actually. You didn't have to pick up the phone before leaving anymore, you were paying the phone bill (and every other bill), picking up the tab for everything, even editing papers occasionally, though your legalese hadn't impressed any of the drab thirty-something grad school dropouts in the English faculty.

And you didn't have to drive your car. You could walk, ride a bike, but you weren't a dandy, you were a man, and so you did drive. I'm just saying you're a man so you drive rather than ride a bike.

It wasn't your intention to blow anything, to blow a good blow. So you kept quiet about Bern, had a nice day; you were lying now—could this relationship become redundant, another long(-ish) term relationship that would blow up like a depressed first-year-university thyroid sufferer in winter? Yeah, you guessed, if you were not careful. A guy only has one real shot at love—any girl who has ever been married to a guy who lost his shot and settled knows this. She knows this and her therapist knows this, the young man she holidays with or the boxes of cupcakes she eats in the office handicapped lavatory, her online go-to couple or her six desperately dreary fag-hag gal-pals—well, none of them "know," but they all sense it. "Female intuition" is apparently hardy enough to survive the hormonal imbalances of the modern (or maybe current is a more apt term?) woman.

Nadine was your shot at lifelong something; order and shared accommodation, it all added up in a numbers sense. She was seven days a week and she made so many thousand dollars writing or reading or doing whatever else she found interesting and low-paying. She bore three children and killed one father and one dog (she just helped him, the pills, like morphine helped him, and you chill out about the whole thing). She had kept a five-bedroom house, alongside one housekeeper and one gardener. She was your one shot at all this. Charlie was the rest of it. Hadn't your first real girlfriend (Helen? Brunette, no bra, excellent kisser—these details you were sure of. Or was it Carol?) said you'd wanted *both* all the time? Never choosing just one of anything, not because you had trouble with decisions, but because you were a dick. It was clear she had something; you knew she did, but it was hard to choose between that which kept you safe and that which kept you happy—and tormented. Let's say alive. Survival and safety—according to the Maslow Hierarchy of Needs, you *needed* both. It wasn't even something you would try to explain to a girl because they would find all kinds of bloody holes in your reasoning and their sound logic would blow the pants off yours and then you'd start gaslighting and backtracking and from there you'd never get laid. Just go along and you'll get what you need to get along with her, that was your M.O. And so you did get along with her (Charlie), all afternoon. And took a few pills in place of the booze that was beginning to take its own toll. And slept for another few hours. Normally you could stay all weekend if you were having a good time or could find a *raison d'être*: the Kissinger logic. He had been a great influence, hadn't he? And as such you needed to protect your balls, which were doing pretty well and not at all blue (or black) anymore, and get home to your real-life life. Charlie was sleeping. It was in your best interest to leave her with some cash and a bottle of spring water (French) and to take a couple of cigarettes (Canadian) for the ride ("German?" you could hear your dead and moderately bigoted mother scold).

CHAPTER NINETEEN

Precision Handling

WHEN A GIRL WHO WAS NOT YOUR WIFE was pissed up and pissed off you did anything in your relatively great power to un-piss her. Don't let a girl bring you down, especially one you liked—keep the girls happy, that is Rule *Numero Dos*. And yes it was a global thing—things were about to fall (apart) as they do every so often. Gore, the kind you cared about, close to home carnage, hard news. Charlie didn't like to wake up alone, pill-less (how had that happened?), so quickly. She was becoming dependent, almost to the degree you were dependent; it irked you, was no fun to deal with.

The only proof of this dependency was a message left on

your (home) answering machine: "Alistair, it's me, Charlie!"

So enthusiastic, you pictured a cheerleader with a sawed-off twelve gauge—and not a sexy Uzi jacked up with the hand that wasn't holding the American cigarette by a young and perfectly jaded olive-skinned Israeli girl. No, this woman wanted to do some real damage. Probably.

"So, Chemistry? What's with that? Anyway, call me back!"

What *was* with that, you might have asked aloud—no one was home, so it didn't matter. And *shit!* your troubles echoed through the library, rattled around the piano, the hideously ornamented Tiffany-(un)inspired sunroom, and through the French doors where the colour scheme got calmer (because it wasn't chosen by Rachelle, Nadine's de facto "sister" and charitable cause, the goddamned nanny-next-door turned interior decorator thanks to a big money sexual harassment settlement). A calmer place to stop, take a fistful of pills and sit down on a garden chaise longue, Guccis in top defensive mode. You had a little girl to manage, a grenade whose pin had been pulled—the situation needed the force of your hand. It was a tight spot to be in, and you needed to be comfortable.

You hadn't talked to Nadine—one of your daughters told you she was at a retreat, working with some kind of problem-riddled persons . . . writing stuff with them, for them? No, probably something instructional—but for shit money nonetheless.

And you hadn't talked to Charlie, unfortunately. It would've kept you out of a mess. You would fix it up, she was one of the two things you did not want to choose between after all. This phone message was just her trying to drag everything into a tedious real-life almost break-up episode. Everyone watching knows it won't happen, but it is scary at the time, isn't it? You were wishing for an every-day-is-like-Sunday kind of moment. Charlie walks through the gate, you may have even still asked yourself, is that her? You may have. She was something, to be sure, dressed all in white, a phantom or angelic surge of youth. She looked carefree and prepubescent—more like a son's friend than anything else.

"Hey kid, what's the story?"

You played it cool, even if it was a stretch; we're to be reminded here that the glasses counted for quite a lot.

"My story? I missed you. Isn't that enough?"

She was laughing and walking . . . no, floating toward you like your own tiny angel.

"Of course it's enough. Of course it is." You didn't ask why she had come to your home, or whether or not she'd known the house would be empty. You could only hope she had.

"I missed you," one of you repeated.

She took your hand and gripped it like an excited child, pulling you off, away, somewhere, elsewhere. You were swept up. She was gorgeous and you were all too aware of yourself—a sick feeling. The pills hadn't kicked in; the darkness was getting darker.

Fuck, did that friend of hers have to say old? And pedo?

But you were swept up, the pills would kick in soon and do their part, and you were handling your shit, insomuch as you were willing to go and have some fun or get into trouble just to keep it all *status quo . . . res erant . . . antebellum.* "Easy Does It," as your AA sponsor's van's rear window told you every evening for two weeks when you were twenty-nine and sleeping with Annie C in the uncomfortable corrugated steel "back seat."

Or, "tI seoD ysaE." But you knew what it was saying: take it slow, man.

So instead you had fun. Went to the summer exhibition, didn't touch anything (except our girl), watched the coloured lights blinking through a film of human grime and grease. You passed the time contentedly. You took care of business and it was a good business to be in—a fine post.

CHAPTER TWENTY

Get Back

FOR THE SAKE OF ARGUMENT let's say a week passed. It may have been less—memory is always an unsatisfactory negotiation. A week of that, lying around and falling in love episodically, incessantly, gladly. Narcotic daydreaming, alcoholic nightmares, French movies, Russian books, triple-X porn and garden-variety nudity. Swimming—not steamrooming which made you claustrophobic. The institutional tiling . . . it was a genetic response; your kind hadn't fared well in such settings in the past. A sauna? Sometimes. But alone. It was a guy-like-you thing (you didn't want to say it was an age thing). You had a very good time, and when

Nadine was set to return you may have even considered, if only briefly, how to welcome her. You may have been eager—was that too much? But you were definitely at least kind of excited.

Nadine had already been home a few hours, however, before you even became aware of her presence. She was doing lunges with small five-pound weights to a Jane Fonda instructional workout tape.

"Remember when you used to have the Fonda workout on vinyl?" You could feel yourself grinning; it was good. Nadine was good. She wore her unstylish white Reeboks and a ballet bodysuit-and-tights combination. Guys have a way of noticing absolutely everything about a girl when they are in the infantile and obsessive stages of lust. It's like diet-love, lighter and artificially sweeter. You noticed, but it was also what she had been wearing for the past few years—sometimes with leg warmers.

"I'll be done in a moment. Do you need the room now?" She leaned forward toward the screen as though she were painting; concentrating on something of great magnitude, the betterment of her ass a byproduct of intense psychic labour, you supposed, or were meant to think.

"No. No, not at all." You reached forward to touch her hair. It hung in a long ponytail, and you noticed how it had grown beyond its undemanding mothering cuts. How many years had passed since then? Say ten.

"It's hard not to feel you up. You're asking for it in that, you know?"

Nadine flinched as your hand moved in close—your dense, fat heart pausing, your gut dropping.

"Christ, Nadine." You ran your hands through your still-very-there hair and thanked DNA, not God.

"You startled me. What's going on, Jules?" She paused the workout tape and felt on the ledge above the speaker for the cigarette you sometimes hid for late-night syndication—reruns of something vacuous, which afforded temporary anxiety relief.

"It's a shame I scare you so easily, Nadine. To be honest, I couldn't wait to see you again." You were trying to reclaim something and knowing that it was not possible made you pathetic. Yeah, you knew this.

"You're smoking? That's wonderful news. Fuck, I could've been smoking this whole time?" You made an effort at being charming, something beyond the rote civility.

Nadine sat, rested her elbows on a silk pillowcase. "Damn, are these beaded? Who did these? Ahh, Rachelle. . . . That makes sense."

"You hate Rachelle's decorating too? Is she using a Bedazzler now?" You managed to get a laugh this time. Things were looking up.

"What's really going on, Jules? The kids said you were asking them for numbers to reach me. That you wanted to know where I'd be and when I'd be back?" She lit another cigarette and passed it to you, obviously not wanting you to keep pulling from hers. "Seriously."

"I don't know. You know? I had a good time the other

night. One of the best since we've been married, wouldn't you agree?"

"I had a good time. Bern died, but I had a nice evening. I woke up with a headache." She accented the *head* and the *ache* and laughed a bit, a "let's keep this casual" manoeuvre. You'd seen her do this before.

"Wow. You don't love me, Nadine? Fuck. You know I never knew that?" You laughed too, not just *because*, but because it was the prevailing noise, the conversation had its own cadence and you wanted to fall in line. You kind of couldn't believe you had said it and Nadine definitely couldn't; she took a minute of serious smoking before responding, which was understandable.

"No, Jules. I'm not in love with you." She really looked at you then, for the first time in let's say a long time. She was serious and kind and intelligent.

"I didn't think it would ever come up," she said. She leaned in and pressed her face against yours. "I'm really sorry, Jules."

The rest is history, you might say. When you don't want to get into the blood and guts of things like this, a narrator needn't drag it out.

It was over was all.

CHAPTER TWENTY-ONE

Glasnost

"FREEWHEELING" IS A RELATIVE TERM. It suggests a certain degree of joy, acceptance, a carefree balls-outness. You supposed you were freewheeling now, but you'd also learned to protect your balls. You were moving without restraint now, and it was frightening. It wasn't entirely necessary to hide everything anymore—and this proved to be a much worse situation than you could've expected. It left you responsible for yourself—what a dirty trick. You, left with your own thoughts, alone. "Unendurable" came to mind. Beating words into perfectly awful little thoughts was too much to bear, like a filthy joke about someone's mom you never wanted to hear but couldn't wait to tell, if only to get the dark matter off your freighted shoulders.

But you kept at it, thinking and remembering.

When you were a boy you asked God for a favour, just once. A Saturday afternoon, a please God kind of thing—let me be better-looking and richer than everyone in my class. You'd heard something. A snide, even sarcastic, "Okaaaay." And you could see now that it had been a lot to ask, but come on, really? What a dick.

You wanted all of it and couldn't leave half to belief or faith. You'd earned that half over years of work, corrupting every executive functioning atom in your frontal lobe.

Either way you had decided you were not going to ask G-O-D for any more favours. When Charlie called, besides it making you happy to have a reason to take leave of your emptying home, you needed a friend.

"Come over. Something happened," she said. And you did. And it had.

You took a copy of Byron Ferrari's latest for the trip and, as a kind of novelty, said goodbye to the remaining family inside as you left, then drove the Audi to Charlie's apartment, stopping at a street-corner vendor for some colourized carnations. Why not? Wasn't it something a guy did if he liked a girl, you thought as you tossed four two-dollar coins into the fedora.

The door was open when you got there.

"It's open, darling," came the little girl voice, not at all being cool or funny, and you thought twice before you went up. You left the flowers on the bottom step.

She was sitting on the side of the bed smoking. She is now smoking, or lighting a cigarette, or putting one out at all times, you realize. And it was a stretch to imagine that this was the girl you were in love with, had been hanging around with. She looked twelve. Her face was red and swollen, her makeup cried off hours earlier. Her hair was little-girl tatty, un-styled and too long.

After sitting on the edge of the bed for a while thinking about when you should pick up Bern from the crematorium, you told yourself to straighten up and wise up. You pushed Charlie toward the shower. She was easy to push, so small and light and tired. You stood smoking, counting backwards to when you'd taken your last pill, wondering if it was all right to overlap a bit more today—special circumstances were upon you.

You waited, and then put our girl's robe on her. She lay on the bed like a damp kitten. You brushed her hair, very much like you or your wife had with Beth when she was small, not yet three, when you still had aspirations of having a normal family. You'd actually still shared a room with Nadine back then.

You fell asleep beside Charlie and didn't dream, which was a good thing. We all need a break from ourselves. You woke up only because the room became intensely quiet. You'd slept well. Charlie was at the end of the bed with two revolvers.

Ah, yep, that's what they were for.

"I can't give up my whole life, Jules."

You weren't fully awake but you could see she was crying and dangerous. That much was very clear.

"For fuck sake Charlie, I just woke up. Relax." You were in no mood.

"I love you Jules."

"And I love *you*. You know that," you'd definitely said, moving closer on the bed until you were behind her. She had a gun pointed at her abdomen from the side and another gun in her smoking hand.

"I can't have this. This is fucking nuts Charlie. That's crazy. Do you think you can live through that?" You were raising your voice along with her now.

"Do you even know I want to be a writer or an actor, Jules? I don't want to be a fucking hairdresser! I don't want to go to fucking business school! I don't want to have those shitty mom-tits and white socks and obscene handbags."

She yelled and cried a lot, and in between all of that it was a good argument.

"You have no idea," you told her, "I love you and I have shitloads of money and I need to start over as it is. It'll be fine. And I promise you I will pay your tuition at DeVry or better," you winked. She did not find you funny. She looked like she was about to shoot you now. So you took one of the guns—the one that was sitting idly as she fumbled for her own pill. You put the muzzle against her head. "Put everything down, honey. I'll hold your smoke, okay?" You were being kind; you'd laugh about this in a gondola someday, when the girl had bigger hips but not-at-all shittier tits.

"Jules, I'm not kidding. You shoot me if you want to, but I'm not leaving this bloody house until I am bleeding from somewhere."

"Charlie, baby, relax. You're upset, I know." You put your hands on her face and looked into her eyes. She was simply young and sad, just as she ought to be.

Then she fired against your ear. (It was in that area). She seemed sorry almost instantly. She said so.

It wasn't her fault somebody had taken it upon themselves to hatch the most successful terrorist plot in North American history on that day—it was upsetting, you know? You hadn't heard yet. You were sleeping and showering and listening to Roxy Music's textbook album followed by newer and not-so-bad Ferry. It was maybe the frankest time in your life; you had made a go of it, even really "tried." You thought of Gorbachev, the man, surrounded by women in fur hats at a press conference, when Russia was a great country, the mighty USSR, and not just a well-armed vodka exporter, and when all the great bands were still together and not dismal solo acts playing for the highest arena bidder. It was all on the table, balls-out. Which couldn't be such a bad thing. Could it?

CHAPTER TWENTY-TWO

The Third Girl

YOU WERE IN WEEK THREE OF YOUR COMA. Your deep level of unconsciousness was good for your health in many ways. Insomnia, anxiety and fear were no longer a bother. No one was troubling you with questions, and it was probably fairly true to say that everyone felt very sorry for you. On the outside, people moved around you. You seemed invisible —maybe it was the tubes and bags and curtains. Nadine was likely in and out, looking after you as she always did. You would want to know if her wedding ring was gone—but I couldn't say.

A magazine left by one of your kids might be of interest

too. It read *Buna or Bust!* A sexy new Canadian reality show in which young girls and guys live the lives of Holocaust victims and perpetrators. In the press photo, Young Charlie posed stoically. What a melodramatic little bitch, you would probably think. She's the third girl in, if you're looking for her.

When they do the Glasgow Coma Scale test they may decide there's a chance you will come out of this—wouldn't that be something? As it stands, everyone thinks you were suicidal. You were found in your car, in the garage, holding the gun you were shot with, heavily drugged by your own hand after having missed a thousand or so appointments with your analyst.

Your wife had said some stuff as well.

Your timelines were becoming messy, but you had a good memory's eye for the pretty things. It's possible you thought about other times, eras, there in your adjustable, courtesy-of-OHIP-and-St.-Mike's bed—about your circumcision dreams, all the shit that went down between Nadine and you and Richard. (You had argued for years about who left whom, and who still loved each other, and maybe more importantly, who didn't.) It was possible you'd thought about the early days with your young children and a healthy Bern. That you'd wished you could've been different, how you'd never lived, with them, anyway, in the goddamned moment. How it was true, yeah. You were a bastard.

Or your parents. The bike they humiliated you with when you turned thirteen, its cheap chrome and rubber gleaming as you tossed it off the Bluffs so no one would see it. The unreturned phone calls and finally promising them you would bring your first child to see them and no, you didn't in the end, all right? Of course you'd wanted to be different, someone else, don't we all? But what could you have done differently? You'd been manufactured this way. Anything else was simply a physical impossibility. (Blame it on God, for not being there for you.)

You probably thought again about *The Magnificent Rinaldo*, the magic act your mother took you to when you were feral and raised by the knotty spruce suburbs that could hardly be called suburbs. Where had it been? The Bathurst Community Centre? All of your boyhood friends and their mothers were there; that kid who disappeared from his bedroom (it had a mural of deer in a forest—you felt bad for saying it looked like a "dumping ground"). What was his name? Lester! Goddamn him! The rabbit and hat, silk scarf and big golden box, swords, chains. The minutes before the lights went out: *This is for the ladies; shut your eyes, boys and girls!* Rinaldo, a man—you wondered if your father and this man were the same species—with a chest and sword and hairstyle. You opened your eyes. Could your mother feel your eyelashes against her palm? Your eyes were open. Rinaldo, breaking the chains across his chest with raw power, slashed at his trademark satin-and-velveteen pirate shirt until it fell to the ground, you assumed.

And his tight black pants which buckled at the zippers (for years likely)—they were gone, somehow—a pull string? Was it supposed to be comical? No. He brought roses to the women, some in his teeth. He came toward you and you felt your mother tense. Was he that disgusting? He was. Your mother was kind and accepted, saying, "Thank you, sir." There's nothing *about* Rinaldo, no charisma whatsoever, nothing that justified a memory. In the car ride you'd asked your mother why she had taken a rose from the man and she told you it was because "he was sad." You'd told Nadine this story a few times over the years, drunk in bed over a hotel phone, fucked on morphine after an operation—times you couldn't remember—and she'd listened. It would be easy to come to any conclusion listening to such an anecdote. And it was true that fidelity was an ill-tailored sports jacket, angry at the seams. It left you flush and annoyed (mostly at parties) and you were almost never unaware of it. But you could thrash from woman to woman and never be like Rinaldo, right?

First off, you didn't drive a domestic car. You had really, really good hair. And finally, the clown had never known anything about true love—you'd bet your Montblanc on it.

It didn't matter what love *really* was. It could be argued that you loved your wife all along; it could also be argued that you were a beautiful child of God, no matter what. But that was just more carrying on, wasn't it?

Carry on.

And where would death get you, anyway? Where would it get you that you couldn't have gotten yourself? Look at you now: a little glory and a bud of pragmatism snipped in the name of the great wild wilderness, life and the world let loose for a while—upon you, against you . . . All those bodies you'd known, those slender bodies, the resistance and the pressure, the dear limbs—and oh, the young girls. *Your* girl. The rest, the mad bloom of feral, instinctual stuff you should have known—those big treacherous minds you feared, the restlessness . . . How many nights had you been torn from drunken bliss, pinned awake with timeless ultimatums: marriage; wife-leaving; accommodation and accommodating?

Your wife never cost you a minute of sleep.

Was *this* love?

The aftermath was a place you could become comfortable in—you'd lived in the surge for so long. But everything had to end. Everything. (You'd heard this; supposed it true.)

In your previous awake-life-living you were hardly awake in your living, and it would be a bit of a joke to think things would change now. You had been a dreadophile, a noteophile and a lover of the bourgeois empire. Why change now? It was too late to stop. . . .

You may have thought about any of these things, or none of them, and other things, too. But these months with our girl—your minor love story—ironically, given how things turned out, left you feeling the least sore of all. (And yes, I know the comatose cannot feel pain.)

It was the most fun you'd had in years. You'd been the best of friends for a while. It was a first-rate kind of time.